Tiny Treasures

EASTERN ENGLAND

First published in Great Britain in 2010 by
Young Writers, Remus House, Coltsfoot Drive,
Peterborough, PE2 9JX
Tel (01733) 890066 Fax (01733) 313524
Website: www.youngwriters.co.uk

Foreword

Since Young Writers was established in 1990, our aim has been to promote and encourage written creativity amongst children and young adults. By giving aspiring young authors the chance to be published, Young Writers effectively nurtures the creative talents of the next generation, allowing their confidence and writing ability to grow.

With our latest fun competition, *The Adventure Starts Here ... ,* primary school children nationwide were given the tricky challenge of writing a story with a beginning, middle and an end in just fifty words.

The diverse and imaginative range of entries made the selection process a difficult but enjoyable task with stories chosen on the basis of style, expression, flair and technical skill. A fascinating glimpse into the imaginations of the future, we hope you will agree that this entertaining collection is one that will amuse and inspire the whole family.

Contents

Two Village CE (VC) Primary School, Harwich

White Woman Lane Junior School, Norwich

Wix & Wrabness Primary School, Manningtree

The Mini Sagas

My Dilemma

When I was three I went to the toilet and I locked
the door. I was finishing in the toilet so I tried
to unlock the door. It wouldn't open. I shouted,
'Dad, I'm stuck in the toilet!'
My dad came and unscrewed the lock.

Luke Peggs (8)
Badwell Ash CE (VA) Primary School, Bury St Edmunds

Car Theft

One day when my family were watching telly, they heard our car starting. My brother shouted for my mum and dad. Someone was stealing our car! They phoned the police. They took the man away. We were very lucky, our car was fine!

Molly Bassett (9)
Badwell Ash CE (VA) Primary School, Bury St Edmunds

Lost Key

One day at my old house when I was ill, Mum and Dad went to the shop to get some Calpol. When they came back, the door was locked from when Dad took Maxey Mouse for a walk and lost the key. Dad had to smash it.

Lewis Gabriel (8)
Badwell Ash CE (VA) Primary School, Bury St Edmunds

Locked Door

One day I was playing with my sister. My mum
and dad were inside and my dad thought we were
inside but we were not, so he locked the door.
We said, 'Mum, Dad, open the door!'
We did not know what to do. We were worried.

Sophie Craske (8)
Badwell Ash CE (VA) Primary School, Bury St Edmunds

Lost Purse

In Sainsbury's Mum went to the machine to get money. She got it. She went into Sainsbury's, got to the till. Mum couldn't find her purse. We had to go home because she thought it was there. She'd left it at home. Suddenly she saw it and ran to it.

Bethany Childs (8)
Badwell Ash CE (VA) Primary School, Bury St Edmunds

Lost Money

One day my mum went to the shop to buy food.
She bought lots of things. When she came back,
she discovered she'd left her purse in the shop.
She went back to the shop and found her purse.
Sadly all her money was gone. This made her cry.

Lateesha Jenkins (8)
Badwell Ash CE (VA) Primary School, Bury St Edmunds

Lost DS

One day I went swimming, I took my DS with me. Mum left the key in the car door. I put my DS behind me. It slipped under the sheet on my car seat. I strapped myself in and I was sitting on my DS.

Lydia Baker (8)

Badwell Ash CE (VA) Primary School, Bury St Edmunds

Bad Dad

In the evening my sister and I were playing in the garden but when we tried to get inside, guess what? My dad locked the door and my dad was standing at the window with a big grin on his face.

'Let us in.'

'OK.'

At last he did!

Scarlet Thompson (8)

Badwell Ash CE (VA) Primary School, Bury St Edmunds

Untitled

We were driving home when the door wouldn't open so we scrambled around the back. That door wouldn't open. Then we saw a door just my size. Mum looked worried, so did Dad. I jumped on Dad and crawled through the window and opened the door.

Kieron Self (8)

Badwell Ash CE (VA) Primary School, Bury St Edmunds

Waiting Game

Last week I went down the shop. A few minutes
later I was coming home. 'Mum's home, oh no!
She's locked me out.' So I had to wait half an hour
for Daddy.
Last year I was on my trampoline and I got locked
in, so Mum came. What relief!

Kieron Smith (8)
Badwell Ash CE (VA) Primary School, Bury St Edmunds

Locked Out

One day my mum came to get me from school. On the way home my mum saw the door was locked so we went to our neighbours. Jono was eating chocolate in the house. When my dad got home, he opened the door and Jono was in trouble!

Ella Boucher (8)
Badwell Ash CE (VA) Primary School, Bury St Edmunds

Ben 10

Ben lives in a van with his grandpa and cousin.
His watch looked worn out. He pressed it
anyway. *Bang!* The universe blew up. He twisted
the omnitrix and suddenly there was a whistling
sound and the universe was back to the way it
was.

Jordan Godbolt (10)
Catfield CE (VC) Primary School, Catfield

The Dragon's Birthday

One dark night there was a dragon who lived in a dark cave. He was afraid that there were some animals waiting outside for him. On his birthday he decided to come out. But there was only a note, it was a party invitation and a card saying, Happy birthday.

Jasmine Smith-Burgoine (10)
Catfield CE (VC) Primary School, Catfield

The Tiger

The tiger purred loudly. A foolish boy about twelve crept silently into the enclosure. The tiger opened one of his eyes discreetly and saw the boy. His friends couldn't watch. The tiger pounced. His mouth opened wide! The boy licked his lips after his meal ...

Robert Hales (10)
Catfield CE (VC) Primary School, Catfield

The Wonderful Butterfly

Once there was a wonderful butterfly. Everyone thought that she was an ordinary butterfly until she extended her beautiful wings! She had a purple background with four spots of yellow with black in the middle. She looked beautiful with her wings spread out. Until one day, her family lost her.

Lucy Balderson (9)
Catfield CE (VC) Primary School, Catfield

The Ice Dragon

In a dark tunnel lived an angry dragon. He was starving, he flew to Earth to eat people. He ate so much that he burst into pieces of ice and the people put the ice cubes into their drinks and drank them up. They never saw him ever again.

Rachael Harvey (10)
Catfield CE (VC) Primary School, Catfield

The Beautiful Guinea Pig

Once there was a lovely guinea pig called Sunny. She had black hair with lovely dark blue eyes. She also had three black paws and the other one was white. But one day she disappeared just out of the blue. Her owner never found out where she went.

Jodie Horrocks (10)
Catfield CE (VC) Primary School, Catfield

Welcome To The World Of Harry Snotter

Harry was in the woods when along came Mumbledore who said, 'Harry, I think you're ready to face the dragon.'
Harry felt brave so approached the dragon in his cave. The dragon woke up with a jump and blew fire making Harry sneeze. The cave then collapsed. Was Harry OK?

Jake Carberry (10)
Catfield CE (VC) Primary School, Catfield

Lara Cruft

Lara Cruft sneaked secretly into the evil pet shop. Suddenly she heard an ear-splitting scream so she hid behind a large cage. The catch was broken. The Jack Russell turned and she ran for her life because it had red glowing eyes. 'Argh! It's a zombie dog,' barked Lara …

Jamie Butcher (8)
Catfield CE (VC) Primary School, Catfield

Haunted

The forest was dark and mephitic (smelly). I was creeping silently, the wind howled and howled. The glimmering moonlight was the only thing guiding me home. *Snap!* I shuddered. 'What was that?'

A deep voice said, 'Me.'

This story will never be completed for now I'm a ghost!

Jack Jones (10)
Catfield CE (VC) Primary School, Catfield

Mystery Explosion

One gloomy night lightning struck on a dead man. Hearing the deafening sound, people dashed outside to see what was there. They saw a dead man walking on fire. The man gasped, 'Leave me alone, I'm your worst nightmare.' Without warning, the dead man exploded and said, 'I'm not finished!'

Daisy Godbolt (9)
Catfield CE (VC) Primary School, Catfield

Molly's House

Molly walked into the darkened house and she noticed that all the lights were off. She heard footsteps coming from upstairs. She automatically froze when she saw the shadow. Molly screamed loud enough to wake the whole neighbourhood. The shape pounced onto her shoulder. It miaowed softly and purred!

Lauren Cremer (10)
Catfield CE (VC) Primary School, Catfield

Florence The Donkey

Florence was a donkey that lived inside a zoo, a very grumpy quadruped that never ever left his room! He didn't like the animals, hated all the keepers too and he was always so ungrateful that he never gave thanks for the food. I wonder why?

Saffron Chan (10)
Catfield CE (VC) Primary School, Catfield

Untitled

Mr Dart was in the shop with Flat Stanley. Mr Dart was upset because he had lost his key under the freezer. Flat Stanley slid under the freezer to get the key. Mr Dart was happy and excited as Flat Stanley gave back the key to him.

Bethany Lilley (10)
Cedar Hall School, Thundersley

Untitled

One day Harmony was flying around in Fairyland
and looking at the flowers. A bee stung her and
took her to a strange world where all the people
had red noses like clowns.
A clown sneezed on her. She flew back to
Fairyland and ended up with a red nose!

Hollie Pask (11)
Cedar Hall School, Thundersley

25

The Princess Meets A Pony

One day Princess Hannah and her pet cat Fleur were walking in their castle garden. She saw a gate that she'd never seen before in a corner of the garden. She went through and saw a beautiful black and white pony that let her have a ride.

Natasha Ellis
Cedar Hall School, Thundersley

Untitled

Flat Stanley was in the sailing boat with his family. The sail broke because it was too heavy. Flat Stanley climbed up and became the sail. The wind pushed Stanley, the sail and the boat moved along. His family were happy because Stanley had saved the day.

Izak Riaz (12)
Cedar Hall School, Thundersley

Untitled

On Monday afternoon at 3pm I took my cats
to the vets because they had fleas. When I was
there the filing cabinet fell on me. I was as flat as
a pancake. The lady behind the desk called the
ambulance men and they took me to hospital for
X-rays.

Clarissa Griffin (11)
Cedar Hall School, Thundersley

Untitled

Flat Stanley was in a plane with a pilot and the
pilot was called Wilma.
'Oh no!' said Wilma, 'we've got no power!'
'We'll have to jump,' said Stanley.
'No parachutes,' said Wilma.
'I'll be your parachute,' said Stanley. So Wilma
grabbed his hands and feet and jumped.

Jamie Livermore (12)
Cedar Hall School, Thundersley

Untitled

Flat Stanley came out of the door of the
spaceship. He was on Mars. The door shut behind
him. Flat Stanley was stuck. There was no air. The
rocket began to go.
'Help! Rescue me!' Nobody heard Flat Stanley.
He was left behind.

Stéphane Rouyer-Brown (13)
Cedar Hall School, Thundersley

Tinkerbell's Bad Day

Bang! Tinkerbell hit the wall. Tinkerbell was going
the wrong way! He was going to her Tinkerbell
house. She had a headache so she went to sleep
by a tree. When she woke up she found her shoes
had come off! A monster had stolen Tinkerbell's
favourite purple pompom shoes.

Charlotte Bambridge (11)
Cedar Hall School, Thundersley

SpongeBob Story

Once upon a time SpongeBob walked to work. He saw a boy by the side of the road. The boy was crying. SpongeBob helped the boy up and took him back home. The boy's mum said, 'Is he alright?' The boy lived happily ever after.

Jack Garner (12)
Cedar Hall School, Thundersley

The Runaway Rabbit

One day the rabbit was lost, the man was chasing
the rabbit. The rabbit was worried. The rabbit
was behind the hedge. He waited until six o'clock.
He thought the man had gone so the rabbit went
back to his big, nice, cosy burrow.

Amy Chard (11)
Cedar Hall School, Thundersley

Sir Lancelot And The Dragon

Once upon a time in medieval times Sir Lancelot was sent to kill a fierce dragon. He rode his horse through a murky swamp and into the dragon's cave. The dragon saw him and the fight began. Lancelot plunged his sword into the dragon's heart. Lancelot rode back home.

James Gregory (11)
Cedar Hall School, Thundersley

The Story That Makes No Sense

One day in a house a married couple decided to drive to the shops. Suddenly a dog jumped out and the car swerved off the bridge and into the river. The police arrived. The couple watched the police pull the car out and saw their bodies. Now they are ghosts!

Luke Young (11)
Cedar Hall School, Thundersley

Harry Got Lost

Once upon a time there lived a boy named Harry.
There was a big man, he was creepy and chased
Harry through the woods and he could not get
him so Harry went to his treehouse but the man
moved the ladder.
Harry's football skills had caused lots of trouble!

Harry Dover (12)
Cedar Hall School, Thundersley

Cat Land

Once upon a time I took Dennis and Jasmin down the drain, where weird things happened. It was Cat Land, big cats, small cats, blue cats, black cats, orange cats all playing together in their happy cat world. I always wondered where cats play! Now we all know! 'Cat Land'.

Callum Bell (12)
Cedar Hall School, Thundersley

Ronaldo's Injury

At the start of the new season for Real Madrid,
on Cristiano Ronaldo's debut against Barcelona,
Lionel Messi slid into Ronaldo which paralysed
him badly for life with a spinal injury. He would
never be able to play football again because of
Lionel Messi.
Therefore, he will always remember it.

Charlie Baxter (10)
Drayton CE Junior School, Drayton

The Girl Who Smiled

One dark, grim and grey night at 42 Primrose
Way a girl lay at the window. She had brown fair
hair and a white gown. Tears trickled down her
eyes, feeling sorrow inside her.
Suddenly the midnight sky lit up with sparkles and
spray. She smiled instantly.

Callum Perry (11)
Drayton CE Junior School, Drayton

Home Alone!

There once was a little girl and her big brother. One day their mum had to leave them home alone. The little girl had found a game. They were taken out of space, they had to finish the game to get home. Her brother saved the day by rolling 6.

Emily Cooper (11)
Drayton CE Junior School, Drayton

Death Is Here

I found a door, it was black and had a big crack.
There was a noise, I opened the door, shock was
here, death was now here.

Aidan Chapman (11)
Drayton CE Junior School, Drayton

Footy Goes Wild!

'Come on team, we have to win, at the moment
the score is drawn, if we don't do something
about this we are going to be a laughing stock.
Come on, let's go!'
Fred passes to Bob then Bob passes to Fred again
then Fred scores. The crowd go wild!

Saskia Rogers (10)
Drayton CE Junior School, Drayton

The Vancouver Olympics

I went to the Vancouver Olympics the other day
and thought I was going to have a really, really
good time staying there. Unfortunately it was my
first time at the Winter Olympics, I didn't know
what to pack. I was really disappointed because
there weren't any long jumpers around.

William Andrews (11)

Drayton CE Junior School, Drayton

Saved By The Curtains

It was pitch-black, many men have died. We only had a few minutes left until the monsters would disappear. 'Argh!' They had dropped a bomb on our base, I was the only one left. They surrounded me. *Whoosh!* Mum opened the curtains, it was all a dream.

Ashley Brown (10)
Drayton CE Junior School, Drayton

44

Zero-Gravity

The crowd roars as the rockets of the space
cruiser 2000 start to ignite, my heart skips a beat
as we start to soar into the cloudless blue sky.
Soon after we pass the ozone layer and finally
reach space. Excitedly but calmly I get ready,
awaiting my destiny.

William Jacobs (10)
Drayton CE Junior School, Drayton

What A Hit Son!

Suddenly the whole crowd became silent as the anxious attacker edged backwards towards the penalty spot. He took a deep breath; had a look of where to shoot. Feeling petrified, he sprinted towards the football, smashing it with all his might into the top right hand corner … the fans erupted.

Owen Gooch (11)
Drayton CE Junior School, Drayton

46

The Killer Tomato Plant

One Saturday afternoon Henry the 10-year-old boy planted his tomato plant. Every day he watched it and watered it.
One day, as dusk fell it grew arms and legs. Worst of all it grew teeth as well. Slowly its soggy brown roots emerged out of the plant pot, growling …

Emily Gannaway (11)
Drayton CE Junior School, Drayton

It's Raining Ducks!

It was arranged. Today was going to be the best
picnic. When everyone arrived we carefully
unpacked it.
'Duck!' Stanley shouted. A load of ducks flew
above our heads. A duck fell down, badly injured.
I bought it home and nursed it back to health. It
was Dizzy the duck.

Camilla Weston (11)
Drayton CE Junior School, Drayton

Innocent Tiger

The tiger lay, stretched out in the evening sun,
grass tickled her sides. She was ready.
'Look!' the hunter pointed his gun. *Bang!* The
hunter sprinted ahead, to inspect his prey. Only
then did she pounce. She lay still, hurt; pain
struck. Beneath him the green grass was stained
red!

Emelye Harvey (11)
Drayton CE Junior School, Drayton

49

Sweets Galore!

David quickly ran into the massive, colourful shop. Slowly he scanned the orange laden shelves, rows and rows of sweets awaiting him. There it was, a beautiful pack of delicious Haribos. Next David counted his valuable pocket money. The total was 25p. He was 2p short!

Hannah Jones (11)
Drayton CE Junior School, Drayton

Tiny Treasures Eastern England

The Massive Explosion

Sammy is a young girl. She was doing a science lesson, they were blowing up things so their teacher, Mrs Weston, told them to go off in their pairs to make an explosion to show the whole class.
Sammy and her friend went to do a massive explosion!

Jessica Meek (10)
Drayton CE Junior School, Drayton

51

The Old Man

Dear Diary,
13th March 2001. There was a grumpy old man
who lived in a skanky old house, who never
cleaned up or had a wash.
Never live with someone you don't know. The
old lady did not know who he was.
He was the first man on Earth.

Chelsea Harrison (10)
Drayton CE Junior School, Drayton

Billy The Thief

Billy looked down the aisles looking worried.
He didn't know whether to do it. He made
sure there was room in his pocket. He found a
rich chocolate bar. He looked around to see if
anyone was looking then stuffed it in his pocket,
wandering out of the shop whistling.

Lauren Stansbury (11)
Drayton CE Junior School, Drayton

53

My New Ghost House

Finally we have finished unpacking the last box
and moved house. I know, I'll go and explore.
Suddenly I heard a noise. *What if it's a ghost?*
Terrified I walked into the room where the noise
was. *Phew,* it was only the cat! *Brrrr,* what was that
ghostly chill?

Talia Adams (10)
Drayton CE Junior School, Drayton

A Change Of Scene

'What a day!'
Shattered, I fall into bed and into dreams.
Morning arrives, bringing unfamiliar sights. All
is not well! 'Where are my posters? Where are
my toy trucks? Where is my brother, Harry?'
Suddenly I remember, yesterday we moved
house.
'Yippee, my own bedroom at last!'

Cameron Harvey (10)
Drayton CE Junior School, Drayton

Home Alone

One evening a boy was left alone in his house.
The boy was watching a small TV in his room
when suddenly the door flung open and there,
standing at the door was …
At first the boy couldn't work out who it was and
then … it was a headless ghost!

Lauren Owen (11)
Drayton CE Junior School, Drayton

The Cake

One day I took a stroll down the park because
I got very bored at home. So I walked past the
park and got up to the bakery and thought *I would
like to have a cake* so I went and got one, it was
chocolate, it was very yummy.

Jessica Martin (10)
Drayton CE Junior School, Drayton

Fear Of Death

I shakily strolled into the Death Zone, my ears burned and my palms sweated uncontrollably. I climbed the stairs, about to faint then I sat down and tilted forward.
'Wwweee!' I went down the slide, I've beaten my fear!

Kristen Harding (11)
Drayton CE Junior School, Drayton

Lenny The Lizard

Lenny the lizard was sitting on his branch as usual,
minding his own business. He sat still all day long.
A ladybird walked past but Lenny just sat, still as
a statue. Several bugs and insects walked or flew
past that day but a juicy fly flew past … *Snap!*
Gone!

Holly Lusher-Chamberlain (11)
Drayton CE Junior School, Drayton

Fearful

Sweat was gushing from my forehead, my face was a milky-white and my eyes grew wide with fear. This was my moment. I quickly shoved on my shorts and sweatbands then leapt over. My gran (whilst sipping her milky brew) feebly applauded me by yawning then clapping!

Hannah Bradley (11)
Drayton CE Junior School, Drayton

Fire!

The fire engine rushed to the blazing house in a blur of lights. On reaching the scene they were faced with a huge orange glow and people rushing back and forth. The fire crew kitted up and safely raced into the burning house, successfully rescuing everyone. And extinguished the fire!

Josh Sleightholme (11)
Drayton CE Junior School, Drayton

Cracker 101

My dog, Cracker, had a hair cut last Friday, she
had her nails clipped and had a wash at Dixon
Center, where my dad works. Cracker felt very
happy after my dad bought her a toy because she
was very good. When I saw her she looked very,
very different.

Nicol Easton (11)
Drayton CE Junior School, Drayton

The Football Cup In The Final

It all started with a boy called Toby, he was good at football. He played in midfield. They were playing for the cup. Toby's team were winning 3-0. The other team scored, it was the end of the game, the score was 3-1 to Toby's team.

Kieron James Ward (10)
Drayton CE Junior School, Drayton

Knights In Shining Armour

I'm George, the son of a great warrior knight.
My dad's a great warrior knight, he has killed
29 dragons and 20 heavily armed men, also he
has rescued 9 princesses, but I haven't killed any
dragons. How did my dad do this?
On the computer of course!

Steven Blanch (10)

Drayton CE Junior School, Drayton

The Big Bang

A man called Bob was eating his breakfast, reading the newspaper. He saw that Pleasurewood Hills had a sale on. So Bob jumped in his car. He was looking forward to it. Looking around it was such a beautiful day, he started the engine. *Bang!* His car blew up.

Jordan Dungar (10)
Drayton CE Junior School, Drayton

Bill Foulkes

Bill Foulkes played for Manchester United and
played in defence. He made 688 appearances for
Man Utd and scored nine goals for the club. His
time at the club was 20 years and three months.
He was born in 1932 and came from England.
One international cap for England.

Benjamin Foster (11)
Drayton CE Junior School, Drayton

Lily Alone In The Dark

Alone in the dark was little, poor Lily. She had
nowhere else to go. Her mother and father died
ages ago, so did her sisters, brothers and uncles.
Now it's just little, poor Lily, alone in the dark,
with nowhere to go.

Paige Killington (11)
Drayton CE Junior School, Drayton

Clive And Bobarina

There was a robot called Clive. He was very
terrifying. He strolled down to Robot Town for a
couple of pints of oil. He liked to impress the girl
robots, especially Bobarina. Clive was forty-nine
years old and tall. Bobarina was twenty-seven
years old and average height.

Joe Hall (10)
Drayton CE Junior School, Drayton

The Gladiator

Augustus was training for the big Friday because
it was the big gladiator fight. He got so, so sad,
today it was Thursday. Tomorrow it was the
gladiator fight. He was so frightened because he
knew that he would die. But he still practised. He
was training. He died.

Imogen Pick (8)
Duchy of Lancaster Methwold CE Primary School, Thetford

The Gladiator

Once there was a wimpy gladiator who was about to face some lions for the first time. His name was Tan Jala. He was fighting but then he saw a black figure that looked like a phantom. He knew all was lost as an arrow was stuck in his head.

Harry Butcher (8)
Duchy of Lancaster Methwold CE Primary School, Thetford

The Gladiator

One day Remus was going to the shops when
he saw a poster saying 'Gladiator Fight Saturday
6pm'. So Remus started to train up.
It was the night of the fight. The sword went left
and right, left, then straight through his black,
dark, horrid, crisp, bloodthirsty, broken, gross
heart.

Grace Howse (9)
Duchy of Lancaster Methwold CE Primary School, Thetford

The Gladiator

Augustus trains to be a strong, fearless fighter for the Saturday fight at the Roman arena. On the day, Augustus fights against a lion, but he's not afraid. The crowd cheers Augustus. Suddenly he realises he wants to be a soldier. Before he can kill the lion, it gobbles him.

Melissa Upson (9)
Duchy of Lancaster Methwold CE Primary School, Thetford

The Gladiator

Augustus trains to be a strong fearless fighter for his family. On the day, Augustus goes to the big fight and he comes up against twenty fights with animals. He dreams of being rich and famous and doesn't need to be a soldier and he becomes a champion slayer.

Kia Byrne (9)

Duchy of Lancaster Methwold CE Primary School, Thetford

The Gladiator

Aquarius is training for his big fight against Romeo,
his opponent. He's really scared because he's so
strong! Aquarius is shivering weakly, but wants to
win the heart of the princess.
It's the day of the fight. He's so scared and runs
for his life out of the huge arena!

Evie Chaplin (8)
Duchy of Lancaster Methwold CE Primary School, Thetford

The Gladiator

Roseanna was training for the animal fight to have
a reward.
The day came and she stabbed the lion fatally.
The lion was dead so the girl drank his blood. The
emperor, Augustus gave her family lots and lots of
money. She was rich and she was very happy.

Jenna Ramsay (8)
Duchy of Lancaster Methwold CE Primary School, Thetford

The Gladiator

Patrick had been training for the big fight on Monday. He was dreaming about winning but then he got scared. *Maybe I'll have my bloody end.* Then he woke up.

The fight started. He was against three lions. He stabbed two. Blood came out. He got eaten by the third.

Liam Dargan (8)
Duchy of Lancaster Methwold CE Primary School, Thetford

The Gladiator

One day Liam was training so hard for the big fight on Saturday night. Liam arrived at the big bloody fight. Liam was facing a gorgeous girl. He did not want to fight her. Liam had to fight anyway so he walked into the arena and whipped his sword out.

William Kimber (9)
Duchy of Lancaster Methwold CE Primary School, Thetford

The Gladiator

Augustus trains for a fight in the arena on Saturday. Very soon Augustus had to go into the arena to fight lions and bears. But he does not want to go in so he hides in his tent. Shortly Augustus falls asleep and dreams he is a soldier triumphant.

Jasmine Bunten (7)
Duchy of Lancaster Methwold CE Primary School, Thetford

The Gladiator

One day Augustus was going to fight a bear but
he was not scared because he had been training
for three weeks.
It was the day. He went into the arena. A person
opened the door to the bear. He didn't think he
would win but magically, he won.

Rhiannon Weatherley (9)
Duchy of Lancaster Methwold CE Primary School, Thetford

Super Toy

After Captain Underpants came back from tennis at the park, he spotted a toy factory, so he went inside. They were making Captain Underpants toys. The makers thought he was a toy, so they put him in a big box and sent him away to a toy shop in town.

Jack Wilson (7)
Duchy of Lancaster Methwold CE Primary School, Thetford

The Creature Of The Weird!

Creak! went the door. *Squeak!* went the cat flap,
freaking me out. Somehow I got the courage to
open the door. A gigantic bat swiftly swooped in.
He went fluttering about everywhere, even the
downstairs loo! Out of nowhere, the bat escaped
through the window. Phew! That was quick.

Jo Searle (11)
Duchy of Lancaster Methwold CE Primary School, Thetford

Tractors

A boy called Nathan had an information book on modern tractors at school. He asked his friend called Reuben if he had seen his book. When he got home he saw it in one of his drawers. He was relieved that he hadn't lost his favourite book!

Nathan Payne (10)
Duchy of Lancaster Methwold CE Primary School, Thetford

The Creepy Forest

The forest was dark and spooky. I could hear rustling then suddenly a rabbit was running from something. I crept over to the bush. Out jumped a poor monster. First I was nervous. I touched him, he was friendly. I took him home but he ate my mum.

Lewis Bunten (10)
Duchy of Lancaster Methwold CE Primary School, Thetford

Untitled

'Dad! Dad! Where are you, Dad?' said Jake. 'I thought we were going for lunch,' said Jake. 'Dad! Dad!' Jake said.
'Argh!' screamed Dad.
'Oh my god, you scared me, Dad.'
'Hee, hee!' said Dad.
'Come on, let's go home,' said Jake.
'Okay,' said Dad.

David Robertson (11)
Duchy of Lancaster Methwold CE Primary School, Thetford

The Werewolf And The Mountain Of Despair

As Will, at the edge of exhaustion almost reached
the summit, he saw the gates made of treasure!
The gates opened, he almost had a heart attack!
A golden palace. He went in, there was a bronze
key. He took it. He wondered what to do with it!

Drew Sheldon (10)
Duchy of Lancaster Methwold CE Primary School, Thetford

Icky-Doo-Dah's Week At Home

When the Jonkers went on holiday the house was empty so there were plenty of chances for Icky-Doo-Dah to destroy things. So he did just that. When the people are out Icky can play. He went round and destroyed everything. 'Home sweet home, my work is done.'

Robert Bailey (10)
Duchy of Lancaster Methwold CE Primary School, Thetford

Ellie's Birthday

'Mum, when are my friends going to be here?'
Ding dong!
I wonder who that is? thought Ellie. 'Oh, it's you
guys! Oh wow! Thanks Miriam, a new Bratz doll,'
Ellie shouted as she opened her present.
'What a happy day,' sighed Ellie's mum.

Jasmine Piper-Williams (8)
Earl Soham Community Primary School, Woodbridge

Something's Afoot

My eyes opened, everything was big. I was still
in the same street but it was bigger, so were the
people! I looked at myself and noticed that I was
… mini. A shadow grew around me and I could
not resist the temptation to look up, it was a
foot …

James Handley (11)
Earl Soham Community Primary School, Woodbridge

Scaredy Bat

A vampire came upon a young child in a deep, dark jungle. Seeing the vampire, the child waved a magic wand and … 'Argh!' the vampire exclaimed with a blood-curdling shout, as he whizzed off through the underground and was never seen again.

Giggling, the child thought, *what a scaredy bat.*

Charlie Coe (10)
Earl Soham Community Primary School, Woodbridge

Pingu's Paintballing Panic

Pingu woke up with an idea: he would go to
Tesco and steal some paintballing gear. After that,
he walked to a farm to do his paintballing. But
he slipped on a banana skin and shot farmers and
animals which got covered in paint. He even shot
himself. Ouch!

Nathan Clarke (11)
Earl Soham Community Primary School, Woodbridge

ITFC Play The Red Devils

It's Saturday and Roy Keane, former United player, faces his old club. Man U going great guns, 10-0 thanks to Rooney. Lethal Ipswich striker Daryl Murphy grabs 40 on the 80th minute. Tama's Briskini gets 10. Ipswich win and have the best team ever.

Charlie Hillman (10)

Earl Soham Community Primary School, Woodbridge

The Fisherman That Wasn't Satisfied

A fisherman sat unhappily on the riverbank, bored of sitting around. As he walked down the bank, he overheard some people talking. Their friend was retiring and wanted a replacement shepherd. 'I'll do it!' he cried. 'So what's involved?' he asked. 'Not a lot, mostly sitting around.'

Francesca Clarke (11)
Earl Soham Community Primary School, Woodbridge

The Missing Treasure

Genesis was a Roman girl who became a 21st century girl by her dad's magic. Genesis' dad had sent Genesis to London to find his treasure and to learn some discipline. In London Genesis found an archaeological dig. She looked and looked. Suddenly there was a treasure box … *yes!*

Callie Hammond (10)

Earl Soham Community Primary School, Woodbridge

Dragons Of Dover

Did you know there're dragons in the White Cliffs of Dover? Well, William, the five-year-old, still has to find out.

One day William was having a walk and ran into a dragon. The dragon started crying and disappeared. William found a crown. 'I'm the dragon killer!' he shouted.

Callum Buntrock (10)

Earl Soham Community Primary School, Woodbridge

Mystery

A circus performer called Bruce, who also owns
the circus, was on the beach just sitting there
playing with his compass. On the beach there he
was, looking around and he saw this person doing
magic. He was really good, he was about to go
home and have his tea.

Luke Calver (9)
Earl Soham Community Primary School, Woodbridge

Golden Axe

Down in the forest was a boy called William.
He loved to make things out of wood with his
best friend Max. Max and William were two very
ordinary boys who'd lived in the forest for four
years. One day they found a golden axe. Anyone
near them was defeated.

Yasir Ahmed (10)
Gearies Junior School, Ilford

Stranded!

'Where am I? Where is the food? *Need help!* I'm stranded on this island. Suddenly a coastguard helicopter hovered over me. 'Hang on there!'
I was picked up by a harness and into the helicopter. 'Attention! We have an emergency!' *Twang!* They let go of me. 'Help me … ' again!

Keval Patel (10)
Gearies Junior School, Ilford

The Fairy Madness

It was my birthday today and I got a present from my aunt. After a while, I felt like opening my present so I went upstairs to my bedroom. I opened the present, but I lost control, quickly opened it, and saw a fairy who led me to Fairy World.

Linda He (10)
Gearies Junior School, Ilford

The Club Penguin Storm - CP News

In Club Penguin, a storm has occurred recently. We have interviewed ninjas and Sensei. No reason has been given. It has come to us that this could affect the population. Gary, local scientist, said, 'It well may be that an area has exploded!' This is the only response! Sigh!

Zain Patel (10)
Gearies Junior School, Ilford

Tom's Bomb

Tom was doing a science project when he flicked a switch. When he realised he'd made a bomb, he felt like a terrorist. He tried to defuse the bomb, but he couldn't. He tried everything then he had no choice but to cut the red wire. It worked.

Asad Mahmood (10)
Gearies Junior School, Ilford

100

Hard Mode

The blood began to spill as the zombies charged in hordes of around a hundred but as I looked around I was helpless. There were no health packs, I was cornered and they grabbed me and shook me. Everything went black as the sun rose … The game broke.

Alfie Jones (10)
Gearies Junior School, Ilford

Gatwick Airport

In a dull airport there were some toilets. At night
a witch used to come.
One day the witch decided to do a spell.
'Abracadabra, witch, kaboo, bam!'
The aeroplanes turned into cows.
The next day the pupils flew on flying cows.

Salman Khan (10)
Gearies Junior School, Ilford

Horrified

It was dark and silent. Suddenly ghastly faces came, weird noises, scary monsters, horrible bodies, skeletons, glaring invisible ghosts, terrifying graveyards. Popping popcorn began, then slurping from drinks. Finally this horrible, scary movie had finished.

Melanie Koshila Mudalige (10)

Gearies Junior School, Ilford

The Witch's Revenge!

There once was a witch who cast a spell on the king of England, because before she had been the king's servant. She made a meal for the king, the king didn't like it so he kicked her out. She climbed the palace wall. She turned him into a rat.

Rohan Mitra Barua (9)
Gearies Junior School, Ilford

Foster Girl

Once there was a house and a girl called Stella
found out she was fostered. She left with a big
cry.
One day some people found her and fostered
her, what she didn't know was that they were her
birth parents and they all lived happily ever after.

Henna Aamer (9)
Gearies Junior School, Ilford

The Lonely Park

Jane went to the park one day, but no one was there except Jane. She slowly went inside and suddenly lots of people appeared. 'Happy Easter!' they said. 'That was an illusion,' and they all laughed, including Jane. 'It's your birthday,' they all said.
Jane had forgotten about her birthday!

Sara Salim (10)
Gearies Junior School, Ilford

The Disappearance Of Metagross

One day in the Pokémon world, the steel type Pokémon were worried. Metagross hadn't been around for a long time. Metang said, 'Where's Metagross?'
All the others answered, 'We don't know.'
They decided to see him. When they got to his place, he used psychic. Steelix said, 'Leave him!'

Inthesar Rahman (10)
Gearies Junior School, Ilford

Spo-o-oky Mu-u-ummy

In the cold, dark, damp cave, where the tomb
lay, was a man who wore a brown torn cloak. As
I glared at him, he went closer to the tomb and
slowly unlocked it with the key which lay on the
sand. He unlocked the tomb and pulled a
string ...

Arthiga Vimaleswaran (9)
Gearies Junior School, Ilford

The Fart Monster

Tom had just arrived at his new house. His dad
was bursting to go to the toilet. As he walked
into the bathroom, there was a horrible stench.
Suddenly a green gas cloud appeared in the shape
on an octopus. It roared, chasing Tom's father out
of the new house.

James Lo (9)
Gearies Junior School, Ilford

Wolf

There was a wolf. The wolf set off into the woods to eat a squirrel. When the wolf got to the squirrel's home, the wolf knocked on the door. *Roar!* And the wolf ran away.
'He he!' said the squirrel with his new speakers and his new microphone.

Joel Todd (10)
Gearies Junior School, Ilford

Surprise

I followed the wizard who had wrinkly skin. He had a scar on his forehead. It reminded me of someone … but I couldn't think who it was! It was like I needed new batteries for my brain. I continued following the mysterious wizard. 'Surprise!' It was my dad.

Ahmed Majid (9)
Gearies Junior School, Ilford

The Dangerous House

One day there was a spooky, glowing house, I was stood right in front of it. I opened the door and suddenly a big giant jumped out. I nearly fainted but the giant did not move one step. I closed my eyes and Dad popped out and said, 'Surprise!'

Noor Aftlaiw (10)
Gearies Junior School, Ilford

The Three Little Wolves

Once upon a time there were three wolves who
lived in a house made of pork. A big bad fat pig
was chasing them but when he saw their house
he said, 'Aunt Bessie, that's where you are!' So he
ran away before he was turned into a house too.

Edward Ball (9)
Hapton VCP School, Hapton

Football Fans

Everyone was shouting and calling my name,
chasing me as fast as they could. I ran quickly,
trying to get away. I stopped, I looked, still
everyone was running behind me. As quick as I
could, I kicked. I scored the winning goal.
'Yeah, we win!' Marc the champion!

Marc Ford (8)
Hapton VCP School, Hapton

The Swiss Roll

I started my life as a pot of jam and in Tesco somebody picked me up and took me home. She made a big sponge blanket and spread me all over the blanket with a knife. She then rolled me up tightly inside the sponge and fed me to children.

Harry Delf (8)
Hapton VCP School, Hapton

Ding Dong Saga

Ding dong! Is it the postman with a parcel to
deliver?
Ding dong! Is it my friend for a cup of tea?
Ding dong! Argh"! It is really a witch?
'Oh sorry, wrong house dear, I need to go next
door, bye darling for another day.'

Lara Cakebread (8)
Hapton VCP School, Hapton

Little Miss Muffin

Little Miss Muffin sat on a puffin and it took her to the muffin factory. She crept through the door into the dark, dark room and then suddenly *bang!* The big doors slammed open. Phew! It was only the men coming back to work.

Jack Delf (11)
Hapton VCP School, Hapton

Alien Invasion

One bright sunny day there was a big strong boy called Ben. His mission … was to stop the aliens with his speedy transforming car called Bumblebee.

Suddenly he saw a flash. Aliens had invaded. He thought fast. 'Bumblebee, transform!' A million laser beams blew them all to smithereens. Result! Hooray!

Finley Mead (8)
Hockwold Primary School, Hockwold

Fish

The fish tank was said to be empty, but Trevor knew that it was full of fish. They were so rare they couldn't be seen, their colour was magnificent, a luminous yellow with bright pink spots. The fish were so rare there were only 50 left in the sea.

Megan Askew (9)
Hockwold Primary School, Hockwold

The Happy Dog

Once there was a dog named Nico. He loved his owner and his owner loved him. He always got his way in life. He lived in a house with his owner Jake and his wife Megan. He loved his toys but he loved his owners Jake and Megan more.

Taryn Lassiter (8)
Hockwold Primary School, Hockwold

120

Scared Or Excited?

'Where are we going?' I asked. Mum assured me
I would have fun. We climbed up and sat down in
a big metal tub. It started to spin around fast and I
began to feel dizzy. It stopped and I got off.
'Anyone for the ghost train now?' asked Mum.

Georgia Wiseman-Lawlor (10)
Hockwold Primary School, Hockwold

Sally And The Mystery Cottage

There was a little girl named Sally. She was walking down the street to see how her gran was. She walked into the forest and saw a wolf so Sally ran into a cottage but she didn't know whose it was. There was a bar but she managed to escape.

Jessie Long (11)
Hockwold Primary School, Hockwold

Gymkhana Nerves

My heart's racing, Welly wouldn't stand still. 'On your marks, get set, go!' Round the barrel and pick up the ball. He's too excited, he won't stand still. Got it, back we go. We are flying. Drop the ball in the bucket. It's in, we're first. The rosette is ours!

Ruby Robertson (9)
Hockwold Primary School, Hockwold

The Cup Final

I'm standing in front of goal. It's down to me, if I score we win the cup. Feelings of pressure and excitement dawn on me. I close my eyes, I must focus. I'm ready. I step up to the ball. *Smash!* It goes into the net, the crowd goes wild!

Lewis O'Malley (8)
Hockwold Primary School, Hockwold

The Easter Bunny

One Easter night I woke up and heard a noise. I got out of bed and looked out my window. I saw something white bouncing along the path. It was holding a basket with Easter eggs in it. Suddenly I woke up, it was just an exciting Easter dream!

Katie Donoghue (9)
Hockwold Primary School, Hockwold

Help

'Help!' shouted Jenny from her burning flat.
'I can't breathe.' She heard the sirens of fire
engines.
'Jump!' the fireman called. Far below was a big
rescue cushion. Jenny jumped out of her window
and landed with a thud on her bedroom floor as
she woke up from her dream.

Sarah Ward (9)
Hockwold Primary School, Hockwold

The Space Killer

Once upon a time there was a boy who had a
dream to ride a rocket to Pluto. The boy got a
rocket to space and broke down and the rocket
blew up into a million pieces. He went back down
to Earth and landed in a river.

George Leader (8)
Hockwold Primary School, Hockwold

They Came To Earth

The alien ship flying above us is very quiet and
scary. It lands behind us on the pavement. A door
opens quickly and four aliens jump out. They have
brown coats and helmets and run towards us.
They grab our shoulders …
It's morning. It was only a dream. *Phew!*

Carolina Ruddick (11)
Hockwold Primary School, Hockwold

128

At The Beach

One day we went to the beach. It took hours to get there. When we got to the beach we went to the sea to test the water. It was fine. After about two hours we went to the caravan and ate dinner. After tea we went to our cosy beds.

Ben Long (8)
Hockwold Primary School, Hockwold

Shadows In My Garden

One night I was looking for my cat outside. It was so dark I didn't see the big shape in the middle of the grass. Suddenly the security light came on. I thought I had found my cat, that's when I saw my dad.

Imani Burnett-Taylor (7)
Hockwold Primary School, Hockwold

Josh's Dream

Stevenson has got the ball, he glides past Rooney,
he shoots, he scores, the crowd goes wild.
Then Josh woke up with the duvet wrapped
around his legs. 'Oh when will this dream come
true?'
Josh slips back into sleep and scores against Edwin
Van der Sar. Josh whispers, 'Yes!'

Joshua Stevenson (8)
Hockwold Primary School, Hockwold

The Secret Spy

The secret spy stared around carefully. He saw a
couple of people walking around the castle. He
also saw a shuttle craft. He sneaked around. He
got to the shuttle craft. He got the engines ready
to launch away to far, far, far away to escape, to
really get away.

Joseph Elliott Spitzer (8)
Hockwold Primary School, Hockwold

I Was Dreaming

The sun's shining, the sea's calm. I played in the sand. I laid on the sunbed, sunbathing. Suddenly it's there, it's huge, swarming towards me. I screamed, nobody heard, its mouth wide open. Next I was inside. it.
I opened my eyes and realised I had been dreaming.

Cain Mayes (8)
Hockwold Primary School, Hockwold

Spaceship

The night was dark, the moon was dim. Suddenly a blue light appeared, it was about to land but it zoomed back into the clouds. The next night the air was cold, in a flash it came again. The moon lit the whole sky. Then you never saw it again.

Courtney Mayes (8)
Hockwold Primary School, Hockwold

The Roswell Crash

The deafening sound of sirens as a UFO crashed.
US soldiers surrounded the craft keeping their
guns pointing towards it. An alien hand stuck out
of the door and waved. Surprised, the soldiers
waved back. An enormous alien appeared saying,
'Hello.' The power of his voice knocked them
over immediately.

Benjamin Stevenson (10)
Hockwold Primary School, Hockwold

Untitled

One day William was walking down the road
when he found a golden ticket with a man on it.
He held the ticket up so he could see it and the
wind blew and the ticket cut his eye out and now
he is named the ugly one-eyed William.

Daniel Bilverstone (7)
Hockwold Primary School, Hockwold

Fishing With My Dad!

On Saturday me and my dad went fishing, I started off fine but then my dad fell into the water. (Typical, parents they think we are a disgrace!) After we got home (drenched of course after retrieving my dad from the water …) we decided it was such a funny day!

Kieran Mead (10)
Hockwold Primary School, Hockwold

Untitled

The giant fire spread from town to town, city to city. It just didn't stop. right in the middle stood a boy, Jim. His mother had abandoned him. Jim was yelling, nobody would help him! His eyes scanned the street. Jim screamed as a building collapsed on him.

Fred Goose (9)
Kyson Primary School, Woodbridge

Goosebumps

One icy cold night I went downstairs, I was
alone. The world had gone pitch-black, patches
of goosebumps and hairs stood up on end. I felt a
freezing cold hand touching my never-ending arm.
I flicked it off, turned round. It was gone, where?
Was I imagining?

Fiona Banham (9)
Kyson Primary School, Woodbridge

No Air Equals Death

My lungs couldn't take much more of this. I could sense the water creeping up my nostrils. My foot was already encased in the dense sewage. I was forced to take my final gulp of yellowish fluid. Black closed in on my vision, as I thought, *no air equals death* …

Alexander Cooke (10)
Kyson Primary School, Woodbridge

Deathly

I stumbled swiftly across the ramshackle ground,
an eerie glow hung in the air, I felt feeble. Just
then I saw out of the corner of my eye a sinister
black shadow gliding a foot above the ground. I
threw a stone at it, it rebounded, consciousness
was gone …

Lucy Collins-Ward (9)
Kyson Primary School, Woodbridge

Goosebumps!

Slowly I saw the sky turn red and the sun turn black. Everyone was screaming, petrified it would be them next. I had goosebumps everywhere as my heart froze and my blood went stone cold. 'Help, please help me!' Those were my last words …

Rebecca Matheson (10)
Kyson Primary School, Woodbridge

The Monster

I was in town, just by myself, without Mum and Dad. Suddenly everybody disappeared but me, it turned pitch-black, then black shadows kept running past. We could barely see anything. Then something chased me. I jumped from fence to fence, but I kept repeating the same one. 'Help! Argh!'

Gavin Davidson (9)
Kyson Primary School, Woodbridge

Nightmare

I've found paradise, the sky's blue with a bright
golden sun, the land is perfect green.
Suddenly the sky darkened, lightning struck. I saw
why.
Men were all around me, all with bows and
arrows. Paradise disappeared. It was only a
dream.
Ping ... or was it?

Imogen Stocker (10)
Kyson Primary School, Woodbridge

Thing

One day John was in the forest, he was there too
long and it got pitch-black. Suddenly something
jumped at him, he was like a twig. It was no use,
it was too heavy, surely this was the end of John?
His muscles tightened, he was dead.

Alex Tripp (10)
Kyson Primary School, Woodbridge

145

The Beast

As the gigantic monster stomped through the city everybody fled. Suddenly a little boy was killed, nothing got in the way of the monster then a little boy squealed, 'I can help you.'
'No,' bellowed the villagers. Then they looked at the village destroyed …

Theo Sheppard (9)
Kyson Primary School, Woodbridge

146

In The Bleak Midwinter

In the bleak midwinter, everything was white as
pearls, but also black as ice. All of the children
on the solid tarmac road were inside, possibly
drinking hot chocolate. A loud scream echoed, all
went quiet, everything a blur …

Erin Hamilton (9)
Kyson Primary School, Woodbridge

Dark Night

One bitter night, Oscar heard a howl so he went
outside to investigate. He heard footsteps. It was
behind him like a shadow. A shiver went down his
spine. It leapt at him. The beady eyes met
Oscar's …

Olivia Davis (9)
Kyson Primary School, Woodbridge

Scared Stiff Literally

I rushed up the stairs as soon as the torturous noise hit my ears. I was in such a fluster I tripped over and my head hit the floor. The world turned black as I settled into doom. My eyesight vanished but I could hear the sound of the ambulance.

Amelia Kelly (10)
Kyson Primary School, Woodbridge

Virus

I'm not functioning. I feel useless. My memory has gone. I remember nothing. I'm in a room on my own, in darkness. I feel dead inside. He comes and prods me, I hear him talking about me. He is on the phone now.

'Hello, can you fix my computer please?'

Kai Melhuish (8)
Limes Farm Junior School, Chigwell

Bad Memory

Rose was her name. She was on her way home
from school. She went to pick up her brother
from school. Her brother wasn't there. 'Where is
my brother?' she said. She asked his teacher.
His teacher said, 'He should have gone home.'
Then Rose remembered, he'd got a club.

Luke Mathers (9)
Limes Farm Junior School, Chigwell

One Good Saturday

One Saturday my mum said, Let's go shopping.'
We went shopping for my favourite game. After
ice skating, even snowboarding and after a hard
day of shopping and playing Mum bought a
Jacuzzi! It was the perfect day but then I woke up
and it was Monday. I hate Mondays!

Luke Cullen (11)
Limes Farm Junior School, Chigwell

152

The Lift

I walked in and waited for my journey to start. I was ready. I held on for safety and we started to go. I screamed as I shut my eyes, I desperately wanted to get off. I was light-headed then I suddenly realised I was afraid of the lift.

Zanetta Ogunsanlu (10)
Limes Farm Junior School, Chigwell

The Young Princess

Once upon a time there lived a princess who was sad. Her dad called for someone to make her happy. That day a man called Alfie came to the palace and did some juggling. The princess wasn't impressed until a man came and proposed to her. She jumped with joy.

Charlotte Tillbrook (10)
Limes Farm Junior School, Chigwell

154

Don't Look

Knock, knock. 'Hello,' said Tom. 'How are you?'
Dave said, 'Let's watch TV.' So they watched a
horror movie. In the movie lights went on and off.
At home they did the same. They were petrified.
Dave said, 'It wasn't a good idea.'
'Ha ha fooled you!' Mum said happily.

Liam Boynton (9)
Limes Farm Junior School, Chigwell

The Biggest Fear Of All

Baker Bob turned around. He froze in shock at what stood in front of him. His jaw dropped. His eyes widened, as if they were going to pop out any second. It was horrific, his biggest fear of all … It was the spider!

Jake Duong (10)
Lyons Hall Primary School, Braintree

Flickering Lights

As Bob arrived home he saw lights flickering
downstairs. He knew that he'd switched the lights
off before he'd left for work, so he called for his
mum. A door creaked. By now he was shivering
and felt uneasy, but to his amazement it was his
cat chasing the torch!

Ryan Treanor (11)
Lyons Hall Primary School, Braintree

The Deserted Forest

Howling wind swept through the tall dark trees. I stood frozen in the gloom of the deserted forest! A shiver ran down my spine, shadows loomed over me. I was scared to breathe, even move. What am I doing here? 'You going to help me with this tent,' shouted Dad.

Shayna Staines (11)
Lyons Hall Primary School, Braintree

Kittynapped!

'Miaow.' The rain hit the floor heavily as the horrific lightning struck above. A colossal shadow lurked above the cat as it shivered with fear, its four legs trembling nervously. The cat tried to escape. It tugged and tugged and finally snuck its way out of the scary dreaded place.

Cara Hammond (10)

Lyons Hall Primary School, Braintree

The Nightmare

Red lights were glowing, the moon shone brightly,
the wolves howled in the distance. I pulled my
covers up over my face. I was petrified. I couldn't
find my torch, I was sure I put it beside me.
'Raaa!'
I jumped, swung my teddy around.
'It was just a dream.'

Ben Durban (11)
Lyons Hall Primary School, Braintree

Untitled

There he stood, a silhouette of a man. He turned
and walked towards me. As he came closer his
body got bigger. Soon I could see his wrinkly bald
head, a large pointed nose, black beady eyes and
horrible crooked teeth. He stopped and said,
'Have you got the time?'

Bethany Manguzi Eccles (10)
Maldon Court Preparatory School, Maldon

All Alone!

I was alone in the darkness with no one to hold.
I had no one to talk to if I got bored. I snuck into
my mum's room in the middle of the night. I
looked, nobody was in sight. I went downstairs
looking for food. Then I heard something.

Alexandra Cornell Atkinson (11)
Maldon Court Preparatory School, Maldon

Family Tree

I woke up and yawned. I must have fallen asleep
working last night. I looked at what my head had
been resting on. It was the new family tree, I
looked for my name. Once I had found it, to my
shock I was listed dead in 2060. I screamed.

Poppy Watkins (10)
Maldon Court Preparatory School, Maldon

Untitled

One day, April 22nd 2057 in Danbury on a road
called Felton Road.
Now you are probably wondering what I am
going on about.
Well one day I saw a girl crossing the road when a
bus came along and went through her, or did she
go through the bus?

Oliver Felton (10)
Maldon Court Preparatory School, Maldon

The Bus

Lauren screamed. Her face went bright red,
her eyes full of fear. Suddenly the car screeched
round the corner, onto the road. As she opened
her eyes she saw a bus, it was inches away when,
'Please leave the simulator from your left, don't
leave any personal belongings behind, thanks!'

Emily Rome (11)
Maldon Court Preparatory School, Maldon

Untitled

It was completely dark, strange but not weird.
As I tried to open my eyes they stuck as if I was
blind. I could not see. I tried to speak but no
sound came. I lay in complete darkness. No one
saw, no one heard me. I was dead!

Aydin Coban (11)
Maldon Court Preparatory School, Maldon

The Thing

It started with the sky turning black. Something
rose from the darkness and screeched like a cat
that had his tail stepped on. Whatever it was
it was gigantic and horrific. People were now
screaming and running.
Suddenly it picked me up and swallowed me into
the darkness of death!

John Kelly (11)
Maldon Court Preparatory School, Maldon

The Mystery

It was a dark night. It was about midnight and
Ben was still awake, there had been reports of
children going missing during the night.
The next day his mother and father woke up and
Ben's mother called upstairs. There was no reply.
She tried again, there was no reply.

Callum Rudd (10)

Maldon Court Preparatory School, Maldon

Matches

There was a boy. He lived in a dark house. The light went on. He knew matches were on the fireplace. He was alone and in the dark. When he reached out for the matches, the matches were put in his hand, a flame flickered, a face appeared.

Georga Bowman (10)

Maldon Court Preparatory School, Maldon

What Would Happen If You Did Not Stop Smoking!

Ted was waiting for his cuckoo clock to strike four, instead of a cuckoo the bird squeaked, 'Stop smoking your pipe and a wish of your choice will come true, for definite, if not, something terrible will happen.'

Ted was so petrified by the declaration he put the pipe away.

Antoinette Rees (11)
Maldon Court Preparatory School, Maldon

Ghost Girl

Today there was a new girl. This girl was different.
She always seemed to look pale. One time I
thought I saw her walk through a door. At first I
just thought it was my mind playing tricks on me
but then it happened again!
Then I thought … *ghost!*

Matthew Byrne (11)
Maldon Court Preparatory School, Maldon

The Ghost

'Can we play a game Mum?'
'OK,' said Mum. 'One, two, three … '
Where did they hide? Nobody knew. It was like
they had vanished into thin air. She heard a creak
then a rustling sound and a scream from the
stairs. She ran. They were behind the curtain.
Then they vanished!

Harry Babbage (9)
Maldon Court Preparatory School, Maldon

172

Speed

'Speed, save me,' cried a shallow voice. The eddy mixed the sea, swirling it into pools of colour. Then *splash*, Speed had been taken out of view, magically out of sight. The shallow scream faded and faded. Bubbles burst on the surface as he sank, deep down to the bottom.

Giles Lonergan (9)
Maldon Court Preparatory School, Maldon

A Ghost's Job

Ring! Ring! Went Ghoolio's alarm. *Ring! Ring!* It
went again.
'I'm up!' he groaned, 'and I'm late.' Ghoolio sped
around. At last he was out the door and on to
Ghostinven's bus. He screamed, there was a flash
and he screamed and disappeared never to be
seen ever again.

Amy Purser (10)
Maldon Court Preparatory School, Maldon

174

Boo!

Alone, she approached her house, ran inside,
bolted the door, clambered up the creaking
stairs, and into her room. She slammed the door,
looked under her bed. Her heart skipped a beat.
Nothing. She sighed, climbing into bed, and
turned off the light. Suddenly her clown shouted,
'Boo!' and disappeared.

Eleanor Hayter (10)
Maldon Court Preparatory School, Maldon

The Ghost

Clip-clop, clip-clop. 'Halt, who are you Roman?'
Clonk! 'Oops, tee hee hee.'
The horseman gallops into the forecourt and
shouts, 'Caesar there is a ghost in the castle.'
'Let's go and look for it then,' shouts Caesar.
Creak! 'What's that?'
'Surprise! We thought you needed to cheer up.'

Luke Ridsdill Smith (10)
Maldon Court Preparatory School, Maldon

Outback Holiday

'Want to go to Billabong Bay Pete?'
'Yeah.' They packed their towels, flip-flops and
blow-up chairs and off they set.
'Wanna sit down Pete?'
'Yeah,' so they sat down.
'I'm sinkin' Pete!'
'Yeah.'
'Help me Pete!'
'Yeah.'
'Pull me out Pete.'
'Yeah.'
And then they went home.
'Bye.'
'Yeah.'

Henry Hall (9)
Maldon Court Preparatory School, Maldon

The Garden Of Eden

The twins snuck in. For once the Eden Project wasn't welcoming. Their stinkbugs flew off and they ran after them, 'Is this a good idea?' panted Michael.

'Oh Michael's scared!' taunted Mina.

'Do you want a belt?' The vines got denser and suddenly entwined, barring their way.

They fell, dead.

Julianne Wright (9)

Maldon Court Preparatory School, Maldon

The Big Dance

Once, a lady wanted to find a man. The man
was spying on that lady to have a dance with her
because there was a dance coming up. So the
dance came up. The man said, 'Do you want to
marry me?'
They got married.
She shouted, 'Yes!'

Zain Ahmed (9)
Newark Hill Primary School, Peterborough

The Haunted House

Stomp! Crash! Bang! A king stumbled through a haunted house. He went in his daughter's bedroom, but she was stolen. He looked everywhere - upstairs, downstairs. He went outside and saw her tied to a tree. He took her back home and called the police. *Ring, ring, ring, ring!*

Aya Saoud (9)
Newark Hill Primary School, Peterborough

The Amazing Rescue

During the night, a scaly dragon flew down and landed in a village. He had come to kidnap a damsel in distress. Her husband woke up to find that his wife had disappeared, so he picked up his weapon and ran to the cave. He saved her and ran home.

Sanjit Pun (9)

Newark Hill Primary School, Peterborough

One Night

One night, Michael Myers, Freddie and Jason
ganged up and someone was out there. Michael
Myers cut a man's leg and he tried to run away.
All three chased him. The man fell over and
Freddie slit his arm.
He tripped again and Jason chopped his head off.
Yuck!

Craig Towner (9)
Newark Hill Primary School, Peterborough

Space Crash

Boom! Bombs dropped from a spaceship onto
another ship.
Zap! The bad spaceship was zapped and fell to
Earth.
On Earth a boy was in the garden testing his new
binoculars. 'Mum, a spaceship!'
Crash! The boy's mum ran out and fainted.
'I'm 3346, who are you?'

Joshua Cilenti (8)
Newark Hill Primary School, Peterborough

Kidnapped

One night my friend saw a spaceship. We got
closer and closer, but they sucked us up. After
one hour they sucked up everybody in town.
Children in town were mind-controlled and at the
end they mind-controlled all of us.
We found out that it was our mums!

Lutfiya Sakarmohamed (8)
Newark Hill Primary School, Peterborough

Little Miss Muffet
And Humpty-Dumpty

As the day was passing by, Humpty-Dumpty
walked to his favourite wall as usual. He had
never fallen off. He climbed the ladder and
climbed to get on the wall. He saw Miss Muffet
passing by and she said, 'Hello.'
Then Humpty-Dumpty fell off. Miss Muffet called
Cinderella.

Ross Hall (8)
Newark Hill Primary School, Peterborough

Rotting Flesh

Jim was walking through the graveyard alone. He saw red eyes in every corner. He ran into a dark, old house. A dead man with rotting flesh stood there. Jim ran out of the house, then it started raining blood. *Eeek!* Jim heard. Then Jim started rotting! *Jim was dead!*

Khizr Naqvi (9)
Newark Hill Primary School, Peterborough

Romance

Tanya saw a handsome man and he was smiling at her, so she smiled at him. Then he asked her to dance. She took his hand and danced. It was very romantic. Then he kissed her on the cheek. He told her he loved her and that she was beautiful.

Bethany Chapman (10)
Newark Hill Primary School, Peterborough

Untitled

Sam was walking home from his mate's. On the way he suddenly saw a Halloween party. He saw an old house where legend says old people died, something fell heavily on them. The heavy wooden roof had fallen down and scarily, ghosts moved in.
Nobody would dare to go in!

Filip Glapka (10)
Newark Hill Primary School, Peterborough

Scary Creatures, Beware!

During the night a ghost was busy scaring people
by walking through walls, when all of a sudden
a monster popped out and started making scary
noises.
Fausta started getting chased by a vampire, so the
vampire could suck her blood. Eventually, all the
creepy creatures killed her for blood.

Rebecca Fretwell (9)
Newark Hill Primary School, Peterborough

The Fright

There was a high-pitched beep and a massive light shone down. A spaceship landed. Aliens came out of it. Someone came closer. The aliens turned the man into stone. They spoke to the aliens. They turned good. They flew away and it was perfect. They all lived.

Ben Williamson (8)
Newark Hill Primary School, Peterborough

190

Space Chimps And Monsters

Bang! The animals escaped from the zoo and took out the police. Meanwhile, in space two space chimps were running away from bladder monsters. But space chimp 2 got a pipe and plugged it into a bladder monster, becoming a balloon space chimp. I put some strings on.

George Baxter (8)
Newark Hill Primary School, Peterborough

The Mysterious Shadow

Lutfiya was eating her lunch. She saw a shadow.
She asked her mum if she could play. She said yes.
She went to investigate. She was really terrified.
She was wondering if she should go back. Then
Josh, Lutfiya's brother, leapt out and scared her.
'Ha, I got you again!'

Ellie Cilenti (8)
Newark Hill Primary School, Peterborough

192

Bear Kidnap

During the night, a bear stomped! He kidnapped
a girl called Katie.
When it was morning, her mum looked into
Katie's room and she was gone.
Katie woke up. She was in a cave. 'Help!' she said.
There was a rabbit and a horse.

Shanice Jackson (9)
Newark Hill Primary School, Peterborough

Horror

Zombies! The villagers shouted and screamed.
Some people died, some people got guns and
started shooting the zombies, but they didn't die.
Some people ran into their homes. The zombies
kept going straight. The zombies started attacking
the houses.
A man got a huge gun ...

Mohammed Ramzaan Rafiq (9)
Newark Hill Primary School, Peterborough

Untitled

Bang! The closet opened. No one was in there.
Hope went to close it, it was gone 8am. She went
downstairs to have her breakfast. She went back
upstairs to play a game with a friend. She chose a
game to play, so they played it and more.

Enya Chicane (8)
Newark Hill Primary School, Peterborough

Fright Night

One day, my friend was walking home from school when he saw lots of police. He was scared. He went to his house and asked his mum and dad what had happened. His mum told him there was a murder overnight and people were running loose from the murderer.

Stefan Paulucci (9)
Newark Hill Primary School, Peterborough

Alex And His Alien Adventure

Alex woke up. A green light shone in the distance and black shadows emerged from what seemed to him a spaceship. He got out of bed, staring in amazement as a green alien looked back with red, gleaming eyes. Alex went outside. All was quiet. They had all gone home!

Ciara Dee (9)
Newark Hill Primary School, Peterborough

A Trip To Another Dimension

High score! shot on the screen.
'Man!' said Marcus angrily. 'I can't believe it!
I've beaten the high score!' Lesley shouted out.
Then Marcus hit the computer.
'Hey!' shouted Lesley.
'Alright!' replied Marcus.
'No, it's not al … Wait! What was that?' she said nervously.
Suddenly … *flash!* They just disappeared …

Reuben Messer (10)
Newark Hill Primary School, Peterborough

198

The Horror

Crash! A photo fell down. Katie went to see what had happened. There was a shadow, but it wasn't hers. Katie dashed upstairs. She tried to phone Cleo, but the phone was not plugged in. As the shadow got close, she ran out and people said, 'Trick or treat?'

Bethany Bennett (9)
Newark Hill Primary School, Peterborough

Untitled

During the night, Tammy walked her dog until she saw a haunted house. She heard spooky noises from the house. She took a step forward. The door opened and she entered. A vampire came to her and said, 'You look very yummy.'
She took out her sword, slayed the vampire and ran.

Fausta Mikavicúté (9)
Newark Hill Primary School, Peterborough

Untitled

'Ouch!' shouted Jacob as he fell off the trapeze.
'Now I'm going to juggle fire!'
'Oooh!' said the audience.'
'Here we go,' called Jacob. He started walking
along the tightrope whilst juggling. He hung from
the trapeze upside down on fire! 'Help!'
The audience laughed.
'Call 999!'
'No, Mr Clown!'

Jacob Yates (8)
Newark Hill Primary School, Peterborough

The Falling Aliens

Crash! As aliens fell from the sky on the bin,
Jack and Lewis went outside. The aliens killed
the humans and went inside. They saw adults
and tried to bite them, but the humans got up,
grabbed a knife and stabbed the aliens. They died,
so Jack chucked them away.

Jameel Rahemtulla (9)
Newark Hill Primary School, Peterborough

The Funny Castle

'Cool!' Jack said, waiting for his tea. 'This is wicked sausage and mash.' Jack went upstairs to write a story. He started to type, then found himself in a castle. So he played the games that were in the room. He went back home and went to sleep.

Ryan Winters (8)
Newark Hill Primary School, Peterborough

Untitled

The doors were creaking, the mice were squeaking and Emily could hear the rain showering to the ground. She was about to tiptoe into the old, dusty room when she saw a big, scary shadow. Who was it? Emily was frightened and shocked. She was too scared to walk in …

Samiyah Rehman (10)
Newark Hill Primary School, Peterborough

The Museum

I opened the squeaky door. It was deserted. I
saw a frightening shadow against the dirty wall.
The door closed. I turned around and back again
in one second. There was a ghost. It was Mum,
blood pouring down her.
'Do you like me?' shouted Mum.
'Noooo!' I screamed.

Adama Balde (9)
Newark Hill Primary School, Peterborough

Ghost Town

There's a dusty old town and people were saying
it was haunted. Emma shivered across the town,
then she saw a ghost. It had blood dripping from
its brain. Then a load of faint, light, white ghosts
appeared. She shrieked and the ghosts said faintly,
'We're coming to get you.'

Jordan Wheeler (10)
Newark Hill Primary School, Peterborough

Simone

Simone crept upstairs to the attic. She had heard
a noise, but she was too scared to go up. She
tiptoed higher. The attic floor was making loud,
creepy noises, but who was it? There was nobody
at home except her alone.
Suddenly, she hit something rough as hard skin …

Ayesha Khan (10)
Newark Hill Primary School, Peterborough

The Doggie Man

Alex awoke from her sleep. She reached up to turn on her lamp, but it wasn't there. *How strange,* she thought. Alex swung her legs out of bed and lumbered forwards on cold, paved floor. She stared around, hearing a bark and saw evil red eyes, forever staring.
'Boo! Scared?'

Cerys Porter (9)
Newark Hill Primary School, Peterborough

Holiday Adventures

I was walking on the golden beach at Mablethorpe. I decided to go into the sea, but I wanted to get something yummy to eat first. So I got a delicious burger, chips and a drink. After I got an ice cream. Then a tsunami came at great speed ...

Lauren Walker (10)
Newark Hill Primary School, Peterborough

The Story Of Saint George

Saint George was a man who saved a princess who was about to be consumed by a dragon. First he needed a plan. He might tie him up, but he's so strong, he'd break out. He thought quickly and he had it, he knew how to kill the dragon.

Andre Williams (10)
Newark Hill Primary School, Peterborough

Animal Antics

Linda skipped to the door of the house, but something was going on! When she opened it there was a dog! How did it ring the bell? Linda stared into space then she saw her dad …
'Happy birthday!'
Wow, fantastic surprise. 'Wow, thanks Dad, I'll call her Sannah, lovely!'

Arifah Hassan (10)
Newark Hill Primary School, Peterborough

The Beginning Of An Adventure

Homer sprang into Professor Frink's spacecraft in chase of his annoying son, Bart. He was chasing Bart because the little rascal tipped all of Homer's beer down the sink.

'You little …' screamed Homer whilst strangling Bart in the spacecraft. 'Doh!' shouted Homer. 'Aye carumba!' shouted Bart. 'Three, two, one … !'

Reece Winch (10)

Newark Hill Primary School, Peterborough

Sixty-Six Million Years Ago

About sixty-six million years ago it was the time
of live or die. A T-rex called Dino was roaming
around the giant T-rex den, when the massive
gang of T-rex's came. She was badly frightened.
Then they started to bite her. But then her best
friends came to help.

Jordan Davey (10)
Newark Hill Primary School, Peterborough

The First Olympic Games

Caesar stepped into the Olympic Ring. His legs
trembled with fear as he stepped into the chariot.
His opponent laughed mockingly. It was 776BC,
the first Olympic Games.

Caesar waited for what seemed like forever.
Finally, the flag waved. The crowd roared. The
horse pulled. The games had started!

Elena Simpson (9)
Newark Hill Primary School, Peterborough

Cinderella In Reverse

Cinderella walked into the dark room and
spoke to her sisters. 'You're in rags, you ugly
sisters. Mum loves me more.' Cinderella put on
a beautiful dress and went to the ball in a bright
pink limousine. She got to the dazzling ball, but
the prince married her stepsister.

Deborah Airey (10)
Newark Hill Primary School, Peterborough

A Space Adventure

I came home and saw a pair of flashing green
eyes. I knew it was my parents, but it was a note.
It said my parents were on a planet.
There I went into a temple covered in green
slime. Then after a long time, a blob shook, then
suddenly …

Devesh Erda (10)
Newark Hill Primary School, Peterborough

Dr Who Went Up The Hill

Dr Who went up the hill to see if there were any Daleks. There was one supreme Dalek drinking water. So the Doctor came tumbling down back through time, to catch it a minute earlier. Going up, down again. Then went to planet 51 to see Rose again. Bye-bye.

Oliver Simons (9)
Newark Hill Primary School, Peterborough

Escape

Jim was panting like a dog. He'd run for hours on end. The police thought he was a criminal. Finally Jim lost them, but he couldn't hide forever. He was fit, but unfortunately he couldn't run forever either. Suddenly Jim heard angry voices approaching. Jim was cornered now …

Nathan Simpson (9)
Newark Hill Primary School, Peterborough

Terror In The Office

Ronaldo arrived at a sparkly office. He felt scared.
He sprinted fast and didn't know what to do.
Ronaldo fainted. Ronaldo touched the button and
fell down. Something was moving, so he ran for
it. Shadows followed. He puked. He didn't know
what to do. It was his old grandma.

Fazil Khan (9)
Newark Hill Primary School, Peterborough

Bedtime

Alisha was in bed. She just started to drift away
when she heard a scratching sound. So she went
to investigate. It was coming from the bathroom
window. She looked out of the window, but there
wasn't anything, so she went back to bed.
The morning came, she died.

Marie Bailey (9)
Newark Hill Primary School, Peterborough

Spooky Graveyard

Rooney was in a dark, spooky graveyard on his bike. He started to see ghosts. He thought that people were coming out of their graves. Rooney went faster. He kept hearing a loud, sharp screech. When he heard it again, he turned …
It was just his mum and dad!

Abdurrahim Ahmed (10)
Newark Hill Primary School, Peterborough

Ronaldo Scored The Winning Goal Of The Game

Ronaldo fainted just before he could score the winning goal and win the match. Tevez tackled him and tried to score and missed. Ronaldo was injured and had blood all around his face because he banged into a goalpost. Ronaldo got angry and ended up scoring the winning goal.

Harvinder Singh (9)
Newark Hill Primary School, Peterborough

All About Animals

One day at the zoo, Amy saw a monkey and
that monkey was just born and it was scary.
Anyway, she got over it and went on a train. She
saw a snow leopard, a tiger, a giraffe, a horse, an
elephant and a penguin.

Chloe Haynes (6)
Orford CE (VA) Primary School, Woodbridge

Charmides Attitude

The guards were silent. They quickly whispered,
'This is a solid jacket with no potato inside.'
'Don't think that you can get away with it,' said
Charmides, 'cos I heard that.'
Even though the guards were in love, they
hesitated to talk. The bars were smashed so she
climbed out.

Maria Reed (8)
Orford CE (VA) Primary School, Woodbridge

A Dream Match

It was an 8pm kick-off. The crowd were roaring.
Ipswich hoping to beat nearby rivals, Norwich.
Finally the match began. Six minutes in, skipper
Jonathon Walters gave Ipswich an early lead, then
Jaime Peters stepped up and scored two. The
score at the final whistle, 3-0 to Ipswich.

Euan Haynes (8)
Orford CE (VA) Primary School, Woodbridge

Alfie The Apple And Paul The Pear

Once Alfie was hanging on a tree when suddenly the wind blew and Alfie fell very far and landed in a pear tree.

After a while Alfie heard a voice. 'Hello, I'm Paul the pear.'

Alfie turned around and saw Paul the pear. 'Hello, I'm Alfie the apple.'

Matilde Ferretti (8)
Orford CE (VA) Primary School, Woodbridge

226

The Lost Dog

A girl went to the woods and a puppy came to
her. Then she was running to the puppy and
hugged it because she remembered it. The
puppy's name was Lilly. Lilly loved to play with
her ball.

Tazmin Ruffles (8)
Orford CE (VA) Primary School, Woodbridge

My Sunday

Deep in the woods, Sam and Rodney were
coming home because it was tea time. In the
house, Daisy and I were watching the television.
Mum was on the computer and Dad was at work.

Ruth Cooper (9)
Orford CE (VA) Primary School, Woodbridge

Untitled

One day, not far from here, a dog called Pepper
was left in a shed because the owners were
moving and the neighbours were not as nice as
they should be.
The next day they left the dog in the garden. One
minute later, the dog was found by someone.

Jade Shean (8)
Orford CE (VA) Primary School, Woodbridge

The Beast

Timmy went for a walk in the woods on his own.
All of a sudden he heard a howl. A big hairy beast
jumped out at him. He was terrified. Guess who
it was? It was his next-door neighbour's puppy
that had been missing for a year.

Toby Hollands-Vanhaecke (7)
Orford CE (VA) Primary School, Woodbridge

230

Pom-Pom Balls

The old lady who knitted pompom balls was
making some one evening to go and box a
kangaroo. The pompom balls were going to be
used as gloves and guess what? She won! The
ninety-year-old woman knocked the kangaroo
right out! The woman was the queen!

Madelaine Thorp (9)
Orford CE (VA) Primary School, Woodbridge

The Ghost Train

Jasmine sat down, wondering what was going to happen next. Suddenly she was moving. Big black spiders ran down the wall. She could feel cobwebs on her face. She turned her head and saw her brother …
'I knew you wouldn't like the ghost train,' he said.

Jazmine Riley (9)
Redcastle Furze Primary School, Thetford

Missing Daisy

It was on a Saturday that it happened, Daisy, my puppy, went missing. We were playing in the park, then she ran off. When I got home she was lying down sleeping on the rug in the living room. I had looked for her all day. I had missed her.

Brier Williams (7)
Redcastle Furze Primary School, Thetford

The Big Ben Tragedy

High up in the clouds of despair where the tall clocktower stood, a dark silhouette was staring at nothing. The crooked figure was becoming clearer to me. At once, the gargantuan Big Ben struck 12. I dived into the glistening river below, feeling my life slip away, colder, darker … *gone.*

Jade Balmer (10)
Redcastle Furze Primary School, Thetford

The Rocky Mountain

As I held on, I critically used all my upper body
to hold myself up on the craggy ledge. Any
moment I could fall to my death. I pulled my right
leg up. The sun gazed at me as I realised I had
accomplished the impossible.

Brendan Bray (10)
Redcastle Furze Primary School, Thetford

The Birthday Surprise

It was my birthday. My dad turned left into a large field and a big sign said *Oak Branch Yard*. I jumped out of the car. My mum directed me to a large, chestnut pony. It looked at me with its shining blue eyes. It was the biggest surprise ever!

Elle Griffin (11)

St Michael's Primary & Nursery School, Colchester

236

The Blitz

The girl lay, while her long hair blew, in a deadly fixation. The bombs hit, screaming with terror, before roaring in destruction. She was pinned down by shrapnel and was screaming like the bombs. Suddenly there was a clatter and a German bomber hurtled down and headed for the girl.

Joel Campbell (10)

Terrington St Clement Community School, King's Lynn

The Spirit Of Me

I look out the window, there's nothing and I mean nothing. It's pitch-black - weird because it's still morning. It's very confusing and I want to scream, but I have no body. It's creeping me out. It takes me a while to figure out I'm a spirit! Oh great!

Anna Williams (11)
Terrington St Clement Community School, King's Lynn

238

Boo!

As I glanced at the golden sun it slowly faded
behind some clouds.
Suddenly a loud yell came from behind my
shoulder. As I looked around my brother leapt on
my back and pushed me over onto the ground.
'Boo!' he screamed, as he rolled around we both
laughed, loudly.

Miller Fuller (11)
Terrington St Clement Community School, King's Lynn

The Creeps

As Johnny walked through the house, the
cobwebs crept on him. He was scared, nervous
and terrified. He walked through a room. It was
damp and the floorboards creaked and smelt bad.
Johnny said, 'I'm sure they're meant to be here.'
They showed up.

Kyle Woodcock (10)
Terrington St Clement Community School, King's Lynn

The Ghost House

Inside a ghost house there was a huge cloud of silvery dust and out from the dust came a shiny ghost. He came out whenever someone said they didn't believe in ghosts. This time it was a boy called Jake. So he kidnapped him and kept him in his cupboard.

Natalie Warnes (11)
Terrington St Clement Community School, King's Lynn

The Ghost Horse

Sophie walked into the dark, deserted stable. It was meant to be haunted with the spirit of Red Rum, the racehorse. There was a whistle through the wall. A white horse galloped in, its mane flying outwards. Sophie grabbed its mane and climbed aboard. They flew away into the skies.

Amy Thorpe (11)
Terrington St Clement Community School, King's Lynn

Suntan

Jake lay on the ground, calmly basking in the
sunlight. Suddenly, a thundering *bang* echoed in
the air! Out of the corner of his eye, he spotted
his T-shirt, stained blood-red.
'Ha, ha!' chortled a small child as he rounded the
corner with a paintball gun.

Robert Collison (10)
Terrington St Clement Community School, King's Lynn

The Fright

Ellie walked down the road after school when she heard a scream coming from an old house. The door was unlocked, so she went inside. There in front of her was a man holding a garden fork. 'It's OK, little girl, I'm only trying to help this little old lady.'

Melanie Britton (11)
Terrington St Clement Community School, King's Lynn

Scarred

Luke had a picnic. Suddenly the park caught fire.
Luke and his mum ran for their lives. The fire
engine turned up and put out the fire. Luke and
his mum thanked the firemen. They walked home
via the hospital burns unit because they were
scarred.

Robson Pack (10)
Terrington St Clement Community School, King's Lynn

Fright Night

The door of the castle creaked open. Slowly,
Sally tiptoed in. The silence was frightening
her as she walked further in. Sally looked back.
She screamed. Behind her was a bloodsucking
vampire! Sally backed away and ran to the kitchen
window. She jumped out. She ran quickly back
home.

Grace Symington (10)
Terrington St Clement Community School, King's Lynn

My Zombie Friend

Everyone was following James. He didn't know
what to do. Then James saw one of his friends.
James ran up to him. He was silent. Then Luke
grabbed James' arm.
'What are you doing, Luke?' James moaned.
Luke was still silent.
James was suddenly no more.

Ross Brown (11)
Terrington St Clement Community School, King's Lynn

Boo!

I opened the door into the creaky caravan. It was
dead silent. The lights were off. I tried to find the
light switch. It was no good. I could not find it.
'Boo!' my sister shouted at me.
'Argh' I screamed.
'Ha, made you jump!' my sister said, teasing me.

Joanna Groves (10)
Terrington St Clement Community School, King's Lynn

248

A Mysterious Christmas Eve

Tom heard a loud bang. He crept along the
landing and scurried down the wooden stairs.
Tom walked into his living room and flicked on
the light.
'Hello, is anyone there?'
There was no answer. But in front of him was
the biggest stack of Christmas presents he'd ever
seen!

Laura Claxton (11)
Terrington St Clement Community School, King's Lynn

The Mysterious Shed

Mel opened the shed door. There stood a saw. It was waving in the air with a black figure next to it. The figure walked into the light. There was her dad.

'I'm just going to cut up some wood for our fire tonight. Are you going to help?'

Ellie Kennedy (11)
Terrington St Clement Community School, King's Lynn

A Mysterious Sighting On Christmas Eve

It was Christmas Eve. Laura was asleep in bed. Her grandfather clock struck 12. Suddenly Laura heard a bang. She tiptoed downstairs, then stuck her head round the door. It was Santa. He turned and whispered to Laura, 'You'll like the presents.' In a blink of an eye, he disappeared.

Kodie Rawlings (10)
Terrington St Clement Community School, King's Lynn

Untitled

Sean walked into the city holding his P90 ready to shoot. He was suddenly surrounded by zombies. 'Damn!' he cried. A zombie bit him. Sean felt dizzy. He stumbled back to camp and found a first-aid kit. He injected himself, he wasn't going back into that city.

Sam Williams (10)

Terrington St Clement Community School, King's Lynn

Surprise

Jo was at home alone. Later, her dad walked
through the door. 'Surprise!'
'Thanks, what is it?'
'It's a mouse.'
'Argh! What a real live mouse?'
'No, a mouse for your laptop, it will be much
easier for you.'
'Thanks Dad.'

Emma Walton (11)
Terrington St Clement Community School, King's Lynn

253

The Boy Who Went To Australia

There was a boy who was going to a hot country.
He did not know where he was going. He wanted
to go to Australia and America but he wanted to
go to a hot country most of all. He heard his mum
say, 'We are going to Australia.'

Oliver Gourley (9)
Two Village CE (VC) Primary School, Harwich

Flying Fiction

Rupert stepped into the library looking for 'The Magician's Apprentice'. As he pulled it off the wooden shelf, the floor vibrated under him. Suddenly, one by one, each book slipped off the shelf and started flying around the room.
'Cut! That's a wrap.'
'Why can't real life be like this?'

Erin Thomas (11)
Two Village CE (VC) Primary School, Harwich

255

The Cursed Maze

Jim was lost in a maze. A terrifying creature
swooped down, its eyes beaming at him like two
giant floodlights …

Sam Poole (10)
Two Village CE (VC) Primary School, Harwich

Mysterious Puddle

When I got home I saw a path of water from where I walked. I told Mum and it disappeared, but then I told Dad and he could see it. Early morning it was ice, when the sun came up it was gone then there was no sun or rain.

Elisha Potter (10)
Two Village CE (VC) Primary School, Harwich

Mouse Terror

Boom! Boom! Boom! Crash! It's coming! The
monster's coming to get us! Run! Run for your
lives!
Squeak! Squeak!
You were scared of an ancient little mouse,
wearing a costume of a dragon with sharp rocks
in its mouth, (how terrifying). Come on let's get
out of here.

Reegan Burnell (10)
Two Village CE (VC) Primary School, Harwich

The Rubbish Footie Team

Once there was a rubbish footie team called 'The
Flying Snails'. The other teams laughed at the
poor, slow players. One player had a dream that
he was a professional. He told the other players
about his dream and after much practice they
flew to the top of the league.

Ben Hawkins (9)
Two Village CE (VC) Primary School, Harwich

Jack's Arabian Night Adventure

Pop! Jack fell through the sky onto a genie's back.
They quickly agreed to help each other.
'Who's that?' asked Jack.
'Ah, the evil genie!'
So they challenged the evil genie to a duel and
won! It was time for Jack to go home. He went
through a time warp …

Morgan Ruffell (9)
Two Village CE (VC) Primary School, Harwich

The Abandoned Sea

James swam as fast as he could but the monster was hot on his trail. It was a race to the beach. He could feel the monster breathing on his feet. He reached the beach just in time not to be chewed to bits. But what was it?

Joel Birchfield (9)
Two Village CE (VC) Primary School, Harwich

The Hand

I was at home on my own and I heard the door creak. I could hear footsteps getting closer and then I felt a cold hand on my shoulder. I turned around and there was nothing there. What could it be?
Next time I'll lock the door!

Alex Khosrvanifar (9)
Two Village CE (VC) Primary School, Harwich

Rock Pool Roller Coaster

Splish! Splash! Splosh! I looked into the water and suddenly all the water was behind my head, and I was inside it! I looked around and I saw a roller coaster with a crab in it. I jumped in. It spun round and round but it suddenly stopped!

Jodi Thomas (9)
Two Village CE (VC) Primary School, Harwich

The Family Buffet

There was a family that owned a buffet and were not rich. They were quite poor so they built a buffet out of old rubbish cans and some rusty metal, and stole some food from other people, then sold it to get some money for clothes and food.

Rosey Pickering (9)
Two Village CE (VC) Primary School, Harwich

Our Dancing Teacher's Surprise Birthday

'Are you coming or not Taylor?'
'Yes.'
'Where's Miss Tithany?'
'She's coming, quick everyone hide.'
'One, two, three, surprise Miss Tithany, happy birthday.'
'Wow, thank you girls, this is lovely.'
'Can we show you our dance we made up Miss Tithany?'
'Of course!'
'Let's dance. Five, six, seven, eight, *clap, jump!*'

Taylor-Leigh Whigham (10)
Two Village CE (VC) Primary School, Harwich

Aime's Pony

Aime arrived at Ian's, a dream pony waiting for her. His name was Toby. She walked down the lanes looking for him. She fell in some mud, got up and carried on. There before her was a stunning brown bay. Aime loved him, when she got home she couldn't think.

Aime May (9)
Two Village CE (VC) Primary School, Harwich

266

Lost Dogs

One day there was a dog called Molly and she was so small. She appeared at my doorstep. She started to be sick and we bought her inside. Suddenly she started to jump around the kitchen. Then another dog came and it was very ill. We kept him.

Ellie Soames (9)
Two Village CE (VC) Primary School, Harwich

The Jellyfish

One day a jellyfish called Adam was swimming.
Just then he got stuck to a surfboard. He went up
and down. Then all of a sudden he fell onto the
seabed. He found himself at home in the same old
bed!

Adam Kadlec (10)
Two Village CE (VC) Primary School, Harwich

The African Plains

This was the scene I thought I would never see
- the African plains. There were some majestic
lions huddled under a tree. It went out for miles,
dry, quiet land. Animals were scattered about.
The sun gazing down. I casually drifted away to
look at the other pictures.

Laura Seddigh (11)
White Woman Lane Junior School, Norwich

The Incredible Dream

I entered the illuminated room, shivering with
terror. Suddenly an unseen light appeared and I
was in a world of imagination. Foliage was sweets,
the river was chocolate and the cotton-candy
clouds tasted like gold. I closed my eyes then
opened them and appeared in my bed once again.

Brittany Lodge (10)
Wix & Wrabness Primary School, Manningtree

Dreams

Kate climbed down into the dark, damp cave. All around her bats screamed and maggots squirmed. At the bottom stalagmites grew everywhere, their surfaces encased in a sugary layer of tiny crystals. Something slimy and cold brushed her face. Kate woke suddenly with her dog, Penny, grinning down at her.

Laura Stephens (10)
Wix & Wrabness Primary School, Manningtree

Information

We hope you have enjoyed reading this book - and that you will continue to enjoy it in the coming years.

If you like reading and writing, drop us a line or give us a call and we'll send you a free information pack. Alternatively visit our website at www.youngwriters.co.uk

Write to:
Young Writers Information,
Remus House,
Coltsfoot Drive,
Peterborough,
PE2 9JX

Tel: (01733) 890066
Email: youngwriters@forwardpress.co.uk